T0289347

An Indecent Recollection

Agustina Izquierdo

An Indecent Recollection

Translated by Paul Weidmann

The Marlboro Press

Originally published in French under the title
Un Souvenir indécent
Copyright P.O.L éditeur, 1992

The costs of translation of the present volume
have been met in part by a subvention from
the French Ministry of Culture.

Library of Congress Catalog Card Number 93-80763

Clothbound edition: ISBN 1-56897-014-5

The Marlboro Press
P.O. Box 157
Marlboro, Vermont 05344

THE MARLBORO PRESS

MARLBORO, VERMONT

"Pride is the extreme form that impiety assumes."

—Donoso Cortès

An Indecent Recollection

CHAPTER I

A need unfulfilled languishes and little by little drives
you mad. A man experienced this frustration with a
woman I saw again yesterday. I was returning home
with a friend.

"You have the keys?" Teresa de Grajales asked me.

"You're the one who took them."

"My God!"

"It's nothing. We're locked out."

"And you say it's nothing!"

"My love, death locks us out *eternally*!"

Teresa had opened her handbag. She muttered, "I
admire how you pick your moments to be funny."

Her voice was tinged with anxiety. She was rum-
maging in her handbag. We had come from the Palau
de la Musica Catalaña.

"Do something! It's unbearable."

"Would you like me to abolish death?"

1

"Hold out your hands!"

"But that key isn't so tiny that you couldn't have felt it with your fingers!"

Teresa was turning her bag upside-down and emptying it into my hands when a woman's voice, a calm, deep voice of a woman, came from behind us.

"I have a key. Wait."

A woman with very thick black hair passed in front of us. She held a little iron key in her hand. She turned it in the lock, pushed the wooden door, held it open for Teresa. Teresa entered quickly and as she did the woman turned around.

"Good evening, Señor Renfo," she said.

I froze. I greeted her, or at least bowed, unable to take the hand she was holding out to me.

I remained thus—speechless, frightened, my eyes staring at the pavement, my head bent forward like a man who is falling.

CHAPTER II

"Blas!"

Teresa de Grajales was calling me from inside the courtyard. I caught up with her in the dark. The woman with the bouffant hair was going up the left stairway. Her thick black hair bounced against her shoulders as she climbed the steps. A friend, Didac Cabanillas, had at one time madly loved this woman. I tried to recall her name and suddenly it came to me, filled my mouth, but I was unable to pronounce it in front of Teresa de Grajales. I was thinking of nothing but this woman. I inwardly uttered her first and last name, "Elena! Elena Berrocal!" I thought of a cry at number 5, rambla del Centro. I thought of the sound of tearing silk. I thought of the bombs, of a brown armchair, of a yellow jug, of a man leaning on a balcony. I thought of our youth. I thought of Guerra. I said to myself: "Elena Berrocal is back in Barcelona, or in Vallvidrera!"

3

CHAPTER III

We were in the bedroom. Luisa, Teresa's housekeeper, wearing a cotton nightdress under a quilted dressing gown, had opened the door of the apartment after we rang the bell and then hammered on the paneling. She had put water on to heat, added the verbena necessary for Teresa's sleep, served it, and retired. Teresa had drunk two cups one after the other. She approached the net curtains of the window.

She sat down on the padded window seat that filled the bottom of the alcove.

"You aren't talking much," she said.

I went over to her. As the names of Didac Cabanillas and Elena Berrocal mounted like ever fuller, ever stormier waves within my memory, I slipped my hand up under her skirt. I found the way into her underpants. I touched her down and her soft, warm lips, which opened.

"I don't feel like it tonight," she said to me.

"Oh but you do!"

Teresa pushed my hand away and got up.

"You don't love me."

"No."

"You desire me."

"Yes."

"Don't take it badly. I don't desire you tonight, Blas."

"Don't take it badly. I can no longer pester in her bedroom a woman who doesn't desire me."

While in the process of readjusting my tie I peered at myself in the mirror. It was, I thought, a tiresome face and I found it weary. It was shiny. I heard Teresa blowing her nose behind me.

"Stay!" she said very softly, imploring.

I turned and again moved my hand toward the belt of her suit skirt.

"No!"

I started out. At the door, I faced her. I stood for some time without speaking. I looked into her eyes and scrutinized the tears glistening there.

"How pale tears are!" I said to her in an undertone. "They're so pale you cannot make out their secret."

CHAPTER IV

When I reached the docks, as I wended my way round
the covered storehouses, the cranes, the train tracks, a
warm rain was falling and soaking my face and hands.
In March 1927, Didac Cabanillas had met and fallen
madly in love with Elena Berrocal. I am jotting down
these memories in the last days of November 1932. In
the course of the year, the port accommodates more
than forty-seven hundred ships. I now and then fit out
a seagoing barge. Barcelona is a port that handles up
in the two million tons. Back then, I was worth nothing; I weighed nothing; my heart was empty. It still is,
but this distress is no longer bitter. I have been happy
since, having ceased to have patience for anything or
anyone. I am forty-eight years old. Elena Berrocal,
when I saw her again, must have been thirty-four or
thirty-five. I remember that the moon, that night I was
wandering through the port, was crescent-shaped. In

spite of the falling rain, one could see the moon. It was very white in the sky. In spite of the light rain that wouldn't stop falling, one could clearly make out the woods on the steep slope of Montjuich and two of the dark quarries gouged into it. The black citadel was outlined like a sharp scar against the sky.

One day, everything you love finds itself confronting lassitude. A man's sex no longer lifts to the point where it trembles, like the hands of old men, before penetrating the womb of a woman. The hands themselves cease to turn spontaneously toward the keys of the open piano or the four smooth petals of tulip blossoms. You no longer meet with your friends in hope of seeing what vexations are ravaging them or in apprehension of the happiness that has rescued them. You have lost the best of them. Hunger no longer digs its emptiness or its vertigo in the center of the body. Nor do the eyes marvel anymore at the brightness that arises in the morning, that spreads, that strips, that little by little brings to light the forms of objects and the contours of breasts, the roundness of shoulders, the upsetting outline of the nose and cheeks of the women who sleep beside you without your knowing why.

And then you stand open-mouthed before the night on a wharf and look at prisons confined by clouds. There you stand, remaining empty-handed, your despair all gone. Then all you are is an orifice open to death—an orifice that does not dream of refusing itself. I sat on the wet plank floor of a wagon, the incessant noise of the sea around me. Later, I walked some more, for an hour, through unlit alleyways. Everything smelled of fish, shellfish, sorrow, cuttlefish, shrimp, desire. I finally wore out the vehemence of the two names and put the memories they were bringing back into some sort of order.

CHAPTER V

They had met in 1926. I am jotting down these pages
at random. It was already summer. For two seasons
now I have been amassing these diary pages and
stitching together these shreds of memory and de-
spondency. I had the essentials of this story from Didac. Elena Berrocal's version was to differ on many
points from the one my friend had related to me. But
he was no longer about to contest it, or perhaps to
approve it in part. Moreover, he was a decent man,
and one who could not disavow a love.

This is how, at three in the morning on that morning in November when I began to jot down these
words, my face and hands still wet from a light rain
sticky from the salt air, I finally came out into the
Plaza del Teatro. I returned to the suite I rent by the
year at the Falcon and ordered a pot of coffee from
the man on night duty. I drank it. I had a pouch of

tobacco in my jacket pocket and I regretted to the point of pain the mahogany cigarette rolling-machine I had left in Teresa's apartment. I slept. At noon, Elena Berrocal called me. I emphasize that it was she who called me. I heard her deep voice over the receiver, I recognized the abruptness of her phrases, just as I reaccustomed myself to the crude vigor of her laughter. Suddenly, I no longer minded the idea of seeing her again. We agreed in a few words to meet near the hotel, at two o'clock, at the *cerveceria* Colon, on the Ramblas. In the meantime, I wrote this.

CHAPTER VI

She was in front of me. She was wearing a loose jacket of yellow silk on which the mass of her hair fell and stirred. She tossed her head. She was radiant. I had stood up. She sat without extending her hand to me, without offering her round cheek to my lips. Her dark eyes gleamed with joy. We talked, we ate, we drank, we laughed. I no longer clearly recall what we said, I recall only that we did not at any moment evoke the past and the bombings, or Didac.

Never have I seen a man suffer as much as Didac Cabanillas. Never have I suffered so much for a friend, nor on a woman's account, nor on my own. But I suffered inopportunely. Though I felt the pain, he never had the help.

Two weeks later, in December, I saw Elena Berrocal again. A little blue visiting card enjoined me to come for dinner at her house, not in the brand-new

11

building where I had previously known her, Via Layetana, but on Calle Conde de Asalto.

It was a large place that had belonged to her aunt. Outside, a dry cold stung the tips of the ears and one's eyeballs. I had settled into winter quarters at the Hotel Falcon, where I stayed most of the time, doing accounts and reading. I had purchased two cigarette-rolling machines, one mahogany, the other a smooth and soft ebony, but no coat. I hate stores, and I particularly detest salesladies' assiduous advice. I flee in a panic. I no longer know if I am choosing what I am choosing, or if I like what I like. I would prefer to remain naked. Though this body I am endowed with, these ribs, this sex, I have neither chosen nor do I entirely like.

I discovered an old building very close to Gaudí's palace, with brick walls and two brick towers, constructed around a vast central spiral staircase of gray stone. Behind the staircase and a balustrade opened up a great Spanish baroque patio.

To the right of the patio, the building had an inside chapel that Elena Berrocal was bent on showing me as soon as I arrived. She lifted the latch of a damp wooden door, flicked the brass switch on the wall and lit up a tall painting, four meters by two, depicting Saint John the Barefoot.

Vaulted, built in the shape of a Latin cross, its ribs adorned with tulips and seashells, this little chapel was a vast reservoir of cold. The choir was enclosed by a wooden grille. Elena took my arm in a friendly manner and whispered to me that she had never dared go beyond the grille. Again she pressed her hand on my arm and nodded toward a chair made of braided colored straw near the gate. She told me she liked to sit there. She could stay there for hours.

"In this cold?" I asked.

"In this cold," Elena replied. "In this great nest of cold. Even in summer it's glacial."

We returned to the central staircase and my back was seized by shivers. We climbed to the second floor. Elena went in front of me. I followed that monumental dark-clad body, those strong ankles exposed under the hem of her skirt.

We crossed a living room without a fire. Elena still held herself as straight as ever, to the point where she appeared to me to have grown rather than aged. She preceded me, walking vigorously. She had pinned her hair up in a chignon. Her long black locks were held in place by a gleaming tortoiseshell comb. We entered a long room that had a fire blazing in the hearth. We sat at the corner of a table as long and, I must say, as sad as the room. We ate a fried fish. When the servant had retired, we pulled the armchairs we were sitting in close to the fire. Elena wore a blouse fastened up to the neck by buttons of carved mother-of-pearl. Her very short, very mobile fingers, bare except for an old signet ring, suddenly started toying with the buttons. She stared at me for a long time in silence. Her black locks fell one after the other from the top of her head as, her arms raised, she removed the comb and rearranged her hair in a chignon. She had a splendid dark face, long, magnificently vivid.

Suddenly, jabbing into her hair the tortoiseshell comb meant to hold it up, she declared, "We never loved each other."

"Because you never noticed my face," I said.

But I had wanted to say, "Because someone else loved you." Yet on no account did I want to be the first of the two of us to pronounce Didac's name.

She got up impatiently. She went over to the sideboard and took out two bell-shaped crystal glasses. She returned cautiously, holding in her broad hands the two glasses filled to the brim with some sort of chestnut-colored wine. She handed me one of them. She drank, standing, in a single gulp, went to put her glass down on the big table behind us, came back to sit down.

"That's not true, Blas. But I didn't want that from you."

"I think, personally, that after the state of excitement the bombing attacks plunged us into, love bored us."

Elena Berrocal placed her mobile hand on my knee and then immediately removed it, saying, "You are always wrong."

"Didac, too, was always wrong."

She turned pale. I instantly regretted having spoken

Didac's name when I had promised myself I wouldn't. She closed her eyes and said, "I was looking for something—I didn't know what."

"What does that mean?"

"It means what it means, and especially that I didn't know it."

"You mean, perhaps, that it was too soon for us to have met, that the moment would have come. . ."

"That the moment would have come! Not at all! Not for an instant!"

She burst into loud laughter.

"You aren't very polite," I said.

"But you, you aren't in your right mind!"

She went on with her gales of laughter. I chose to sit on the gray and very warm slab of the hearth. I lit a cigarette and wet my lips in the alcohol she had served me. Long locks kept slipping from what was left of her chignon and their motion made her even more beautiful. She was twisting the gleaming locks between her fingers. Elena Berrocal calmed down. She said, "In any case, a thousand years or a thousand leagues of distance are nothing to those who are meant to meet."

I thought for a moment. I said, "Chance, desire, fear, and death leave men and women face to face."

She said, "Chance, desire, fear, and life leave them alone."

CHAPTER VII

In 1928, I had left Barcelona for the socialist circles of
Berlin. I hadn't seen her again. I spoke of Ottwalt, of
Benn, whom she knew personally. She asked me if I
had seen *The Blue Angel*. I told her that I hadn't seen
it. She shrugged. She said, "It's a pity."

Then she added that it didn't interest her anymore.

"Blas, I owe you the foundation my life stands on."

"Elena, you don't owe me anything."

"Nevertheless I'm going to tell you."

She paused. I didn't question her. Her fingers played
with her hair: they were red and gilded by the blazing
fire. I bent over and pushed the logs closer together. I
remembered the young woman she had been, anarchist, terrorist—terrified too, pious too—whose confidences had always been strange. Her confidences
disconcerted me every time. We had seen each other
naked once, by chance, in the kitchen of the apart-

16

ment where we were hiding. It was the middle of the night. We were anxious, both feeling sick to our stomachs; we had run into each other in front of the door to the toilet. Another time, opening the door of a garage, I had come upon this young woman who believed in nothing, who wanted without further delay to bathe Primo de Rivera's orgies in blood, suddenly on her knees, in her work clothes, preparing the fuse of a bomb, wringing her fingers and praying.

In those moments, she would claim that God had not withdrawn from the world without leaving traces behind. But according to her, he had left none in the nature of man. He had left some in the course of rivers, in nightmares, among lizards, and in the obscurity that daily turns into darkness.

Suddenly, in her deep voice, and with the strange and unexpected aid of her laughter, she said, "It's a nasty story!"

I raised my eyes toward her.

"Very nasty," Elena repeated.

"I don't believe you are nasty. If there is one thing I believe," I said, "it's that you are not nasty."

She stopped looking at me. She was musing, her head lay back, her neck against the edge of the wooden armchair she was sitting in. Her voice grew quieter and deeper. She said slowly, "It's madness to believe that it lies within your power to make yourself happy through the control you exert over your thoughts. You are not free to think as you like. You aren't free to love as you like. If you must submit to a certain kind of pleasure that suits your nature, I can swear to you that there is no happiness in resigning yourself to it. The pleasure that tears the most intense joy from us is sometimes a prison in which we suffer."

Ruffling her hair with her hands, she gave me a glance full of anxiety. Then she looked at the dark window facing her. She continue, "I hated Gaspar Guerra's mind. He was a politician. He spent his time praising Catalan coral, Valencia silk, Seville soap, man's goodness, Toledo stockings. His face and hands were magnificent. I didn't like his bony, avid body. Furthermore, the form his desire took revolted me. He would fall on me certain nights and every morning without exception. It was a spasm that hurt me and that didn't fetch a sound from him unless it was a sort of hiccough. He washed himself in a tub afterward. His white skin looked like curdled milk. But his hair and all the black hair on his body was as soft as crows' feathers.

"We had loved each other without there having been any love. We left each other, however, in sorrow and in hatred. I stayed alone for about a year. I went out with Juan, but Guerra would come by unexpectedly. His resentment and his suffering did not diminish. Not only, according to him, was his suffering not diminishing, but it was increasing, and he blamed me for it as if I were devoting my time to increasing his suffering. I am always amazed by men's dishonesty.

He maintained that his feelings for me had changed into a powerful desire that neither distance, nor solitude, nor wine drunk to excess, nor other women could appease. One morning, after I had spent the night with Juan, getting up to go piss, crossing the living room, I discovered him near the fireplace, shaking by the marble mantelpiece of the fireplace in a flannel suit soaked with rain. The fireplace contained neither wood nor embers; it's true that this spot, then incapable of warming him, had always been where he had launched into his most eloquent speeches. He had never consented to give me back the keys to my apartment. Little by little, the place became distasteful to me, and that is one of the reasons I bought, around that time, the house in Vallvidrera.

"I went to fetch some dry clothes because he had no intention of moving from the spot where he stood shivering. He refused to speak to me. He undressed in front of me. I remember that his penis was tiny and ridiculous. I caught a glimpse of it in the shadows. I showed him to the door, pushing and pulling, went back to my room, and told Juan not to ask me any questions and kindly to leave too, immediately. Half awake, dazed, Juan got dressed. I threw him out without his understanding why. I got back into bed alone, pulled the sheet up to my chin, and was finally able, if not to cry, to let out sobs— dry sobs, as dry as my pleasures, but that racked me as though they had been true tears.

19

"I didn't sleep. At noon I decided to leave. Climbing aboard the train, I remember commenting to myself that to break with a man whom you no longer love, whom you despise intellectually, and who never gave you any physical pleasure, still makes you suffer a great deal.

"I went to Berlin and lived there for four months. It's true that I was very close to Gottfried Benn."

CHAPTER VIII

"Upon my return here, I resumed a fuller social life. We went to dinner with everyone who shared our political views and thus inevitably ran into Gaspar Guerra. We went to Alcalá Zamora's, to Maciá's. I did all I could to turn those evenings into veritable riots. If he was there, I provoked him. He no longer answered me. I read pain on his face, but this pain itself exasperated me. It was at Maciá's that I met Didac Cabanillas. He was as subtle as Guerra was ambitious; as considerate as Guerra had been indifferent to what I might be thinking or dreaming; as cultured, as affable, as Gaspar Guerra was insensible to anything outside of force and secrecy. Didac moved in with me, into the apartment on Via Layetana you once knew. I was no longer much inclined to allow a man's will to decide how my life was to be run. I have never come in a man's arms. From me they fetch only a trickle. It's of the sea I've always dreamt.

"The first time I saw Didac, the two of them were side by side. Didac Cabanillas, holding Guerra's ferocious thinness by the arm, was wearing a blue suit. In contrast, there was a certain fullness to him, a suggestion of breadth in the way he carried himself. His sex was rather substantial. He was very attractive.

"I must have met him for the first time in March or April of 1927. I remember that it was spring, after my return from Berlin. I remember that I had bought the villa in Vallvidrera. It was before I had the work done on it. It was well before Maciá's election, three or four years before Maciá's speech. You remember the balcony of the Disputación.

"Didac loved the painting of the Baroque artists and Zurbarán. He loved music. It was a change from Gaspar Guerra and Juan's invisibility. Didac was more or less the friend of Miguel de Unamuno; he introduced me to Webern. He was not tall. His arms, his neck, his shoulders were distinctly developed. His face was framed by short curly hair. You remember that he wore sideburns. The hips were narrower, even though the thighs were muscular. His feet were small. When he was silent, he was a courteous man, attentive, and even absorbed. When he spoke, his countenance at once lit up. His features were complex, often contradictory; his nose was crooked, he had great circles under his eyes. His language was beautiful, it contained a touch of the cynical but it was joyous, puritan and often old-fashioned, but full of charm. It was this *joie de vivre* of his that attracted me to him, and the quality of his clothes. I have little taste for women's clothes but I appreciate it when a man is well-dressed and never speaks of these things. You, for instance, you have never been well-dressed. He danced reasonably well, with his feet pointing in a little, but without awkwardness. This touched me. I adored dancing. He held himself well. His torso was broad, his back always straight. He gave the impression of self-confident ease.

"Gaspar Guerra pestered me again when he was informed of our affair. Yet we hadn't flaunted it; I was insistent about that. He came straight up to me, asked me the question. I shrugged by way of denial. Without a word he slapped me, with the same determination that he applied to his career, that enabled him to succeed, and that impelled him when he led the Generalitat to the immense shabby mess he left it in.

"There was a clock standing near me on the mantel of the fireplace and I pushed it over on him, without saying a word either; it landed on his foot. He let out a howl. But we said nothing further to one another, and it was limping and his face white with pain that he left the living room. It was in silence, all conversation having abruptly ceased, that our relations came to what turned out to be a defintive end.

"To the same extent that Gaspar Guerra had promoted Didac—he had made him his right-hand man—he now sought to bring him down and discredit him among our friends. He went around saying that Didac Cabanillas was Ramon del Valle-Inclán's *left-hand man.*

"Didac liked to talk and go out. When he handed over his hat and coat and walked into a living room, he was happy; he grew even more attractive. To tell the truth, he was never gloomy, whereas I for my part so often was. I am inclined to dominate and if the effect of things is to constrain me, I am immediately annoyed and become unpleasant or unhappy for hours. He showed me a thousand little kindnesses when I was depressed and weary, and he excused my sadness by invoking the passion I showed for generous causes and for humiliated mankind, by invoking the vivacity of my angers, the tenaciousness of my hostility, the ardor I generally put into everything I undertook.

"Didac drank, but not to excess. He was a great smoker, but he would open the windows. He preferred talking to playing cards and I preferred a million times more to play cards than to talk. He wasn't wealthy but at the Yepes bank earned more than enough to live on. Before going to his office, he would read for an hour—Unamuno's books, Machado's poems, he would say, but in truth what he read was novels. I prefered Karl Schmitt or Benn and tried to

24

whisper those names in his ear. He had a mistress with no social standing and without very much going on in her head who had three grown children he had gotten to adore him. That was how he had seduced her, but he never told me anything else because I had declared to him that I might not give myself to a man right away but that I was exclusive. And that I would not put up with this relationship if he had ever considered going on with it.

"He broke with this woman without being asked twice. I believe he thought of making me his wife. But I think that my virulence on the subject of marriage and my sensitivity about any form of subordination dissuaded him from proposing to me.

"In painting, I saw with my own eyes and what they saw was beautiful. In music, I trusted his ear completely. On politics and literature, we diverged; clothes and furniture, we thought alike. Going out with him to buy anything whatsoever was an unclouded joy. We would silently agree in front of a sofa or a screen or a secretary. We liked to go out with each other. We were as thick as thieves.

"I was seeking anything then that might serve as a fuse to destroy the pig's dictatorship. It was at this time that I received from Berlin the first copy of Martin Heidegger's *Sein und Zeit*, the off-print of Sigmund Freud's "Der Humor," from the *Almanach*, and Karl Schmitt's *Political Primer* which disappointed me because the theses he defended were far less radical than those in his *Political Theology*. 'All domestic politics are a phantom civil war'—we knew that by heart. My Berlin friends were especially urging me to read Martin Heidegger. I read him with so much fervor that I can maintain that the reading of a book altered my life. What I liked in religion were credulities as legendary as they were fanatical, and I had come upon a theologian whose approach to everything was startlingly unusual. I gave it to Didac to read, who found the work difficult and didn't have the same impression as I. He was hardly overwhelmed by it and even later confided to me that he had given up reading it after ten pages. I was disappointed and along with my disappointment felt a little bit of scorn.

"It was at the same time that one of Gaspar Guerra's secretaries had the May note brought to me. I went to his house the next day at six o'clock. I found about seventy members of the opposition there, gathered around a number of tables lined up end to end, with oil lamps and glasses of water to which lemon had been added. Thirty meters from me sat Didac Cabanillas; he was on Guerra's left. You, you were on his right. It was there, amidst dead silence, that Guerra read the letter Macià had written. Our hearts were beating with enthusiasm when the gathering broke up, even if fear could be detected in the depths of our gazes. It was perceptible, notably on your face.

"Didac joined me later in my apartment. I was changing. When I returned to the living room, I found him perched on the edge of the little sofa that we had bought together and placed in the chimney corner. He looked downcast. He was taking off his soaked boots in front of the copper screen meant to prevent flying sparks, which he had also bought. These screens are ugly and absurd. They are a man's idea.

"In my opinion, the only protection from fire is burning.

"He put down his boots, rose, rushed toward me, took me by the shoulders, pulled me to him, and pressed his lips against mine. His erection bulged the fabric of his pants. Without leaving him a moment, I thrust him away, pressing the flat of my hand against his belly. I said firmly, " 'It is out of the question that I ever desire your desire in this form.'

"He had been drinking. He suggested that he was going to leave the apartment, resume the life he had led up until then, which had made him happy, return to his home, and put more distance between our ways of living, since I wished it so. I retorted that he was absolutely free to do as he pleased, but that in that case we would not see each other again. He had the face of a man full of rage but threatening to cry, the bags under his eyes all round and sagging, and was spluttering I don't know what about desire. I told him that women had ceased to be slaves, and above all ceased to be guilty ones. I was full of fury. He did budge. He stayed in my apartment.

"Another evening, we were going to the Liceo to

see Gluck's *Orfeo*, an opera I'm far from admiring. It was hot. In the lobby, in front of the counter where you pick up your tickets, I pulled away my hand, which he had taken and was clutching. He asked me why. We were going up the stairs that lead to the balcony. I stopped him and said to him, very softly and looking him in the eyes, slowly pronouncing the syllables:

" 'I only like one thing, Didac: to have a finger put all the way inside my ass when there are people nearby. Then the sluices open, without it showing on my face. Not on the ground, you have my word.'

"He was taken aback. Didac immediately looked about him, anxiously observing the people around us. He tried to continue on up the stairs. I held him back by the arm.

" 'You seem puzzled, Didac, especially for a man who claims he desires me. I understand that the proceeding may seem embarrassing. I am also aware that it doesn't provide much satisfaction for the one who procures me this pleasure.'

"Didac looked panic-stricken. It was sheer provocation on my part. He had taken my elbow and wanted us to continue up the marble staircase. He said to me, 'You're putting me in an incredible situation.'

" 'Let's subscribe to this treaty, Didac Cabanillas. You make me come nine times in this way, and then— only then—will I give myself to you.'

"We were blocking the way of those who wanted to pass. He wanted at all costs to go up and find our box. He was as red as a lobster. I wrenched my elbow from his hand. I took his chin in my right hand and forced him to look me in the eyes. I told him that he was perhaps a coward and that the idea of being caught in the act undoubtedly frightened him far more than my body aroused his lust. He denied it, shook his head no several times, again tried to go up. He gave the excuse that he didn't trust the bargain I was offering him, that he feared I would always refuse myself to him, and that he could not commit himself to being so eternally patient. That arousal could drive one raving mad. That these games I was asking him to play, because they were more in the realm of childishness than of pleasure, did not transport him and bore little relation to his idea of love. I shrugged my shoulders and, pointing at his crotch, said to him: " 'When one sees, Señor Cabanillas, what one sees from your pants, I say to myself that the way in which I am envisaging taking pleasure does not repel you as keenly as you claim it does.'

"And I walked ahead of him."

CHAPTER IX

"I loved using crude words. I still love them. He was lost, like a child. It was a long time before he took to this freedom I had in the use of language, this freedom to speak without lying. Then he felt the joy that brightens in the mind from never duping oneself with words. He came to know the jubilation, also, that the entire body feels when the mouth slowly utters expressions that are ordinarily not permitted, and when you pronounce them deliberately, firmly, to render them still less tolerable.

"I have sometimes thought that in the morning, before he left for his bank, he must have read, rather than Martin Heidegger, the novels of Joaquin Belda. They are the shame of the whole of Spain, to the extent a 'whole of Spain' exists on this earth.

"That evening, I left him at the first intermission, without his having said a word. I had taken his hand in the dark and placed it on my thigh, and he had immediately removed it. I left him to that affected story in which a man prefers to lose a woman to death, turning back toward her to assure himself that she is beautiful and that so much beauty will plunge rivals, family, former mistresses, even mirrors into envy, rather than to share fear with her and forge ahead side by side toward the unknown fire that burns where days end.

"Two days later, he was at my apartment. I did not mention the conversation we had had on the steps leading up to the theater boxes. He told me that he preferred to live at his place again, but that for nothing in the world would he sacrifice his need to see me and talk to me. I sighed that perhaps I was not a need. Did he look upon women as chamber pots? I've never been affectionate. I've never been satisfied by anything. Didac had a generous soul and he liked to give. At least he was prodigal to any person who seemed proud to him. From the instant you were fierce and had a passionate taste for anything in the world whatsoever, he was immediately indebted to you and forgave you everything so long as you allowed him to enter your passion and welcomed him there. It is true I soon realized that he was only so obliging because he was obsessed with the desire to provoke occasions to prove it. He also had this curious trait of blowing on every fire he came close to while pretending to want to quiet it down. He fuelled atmospheres of quarrelings, of outcries, of spilled blood, so as to be able to figure in the fine role of the victim's savior. He noticed everyone's tastes, immediately filed them away in a corner of his memory, and the rest of the time went to all sorts of trouble to satisfy them. This sometimes roused my bad temper. There wasn't a soup, a flower, a fish, a perfume, an ice cream, a wine, a cigar, a hat, a sweet that he didn't pluck out of his hat with a regularity that little by little became burdensome. I often told him he might cherish my tastes less and me more. And that he might worry about my happiness rather than keeping an inventory of my divers likes and dislikes. But he never let go of this need to oblige, and he wearied of me before he tired of bringing me wheels of brie and yellow tulips.

"Such an obliging man could not fail to consider satisfying the sexual whims of the woman he loved. Didac suddenly told me that he consented to what I was asking him to do."

CHAPTER X

"When Didac Cabanillas told me that he agreed to what I requested, I was most surprised.

"I had never avowed this desire to anyone. I had been led on mainly by the pleasure I took in disconcerting him. We decided that it would be at the Liceo, in a box. We were to hear a Monteverdi opera, in Westrup's version. Didac had taught me to like this music. We were in February. On the evening before, I had qualms and wanted to dismiss this fantasy forever. I telephoned Didac; he was not home. The excitement of the night spent alone in my bed, the certainty, pretty much shared by our species, that the duration of human life is not long, or rather the cold dread of the poverty and the brevity of the days death allows us, the pleasure of commiting the offense, and especially the propriety, the affliction, the embarrassment, the friendship, and the secrecy of the one who would procure me this emotion finally removed my scruples, without freeing me from the uneasiness they were accompanied by. I rose at dawn both exhausted and determined.

"I have the most volatile disposition. A cloud in the sky when I am eager to go out, a layer of dust I discover on a piece of furniture, a servant's whisper behind my back can annoy me and throw me into a state of chiliness and peevish animosity for the entire day. An awkward gesture, an ill-placed piece of kindling that causes the newly-built fire to collapse all aheap are apt to make me as gay as a clown and inspire me to obligingness worthy of a French lover.

"I remember that my father, taking his penknife from the pocket of his jacket, used to cut a cube from the bar of soap and taper it with the tip of the blade, force me to lie on my belly, spread my buttocks, and shove in his improvised suppository to bring an end to a two-day-long constipation. You can understand my hatred for Primo de Rivera's dictatorship. I suspect that your rebellion probably didn't stem from any nobler motives. Christianity happens to be the only religion in which God has taken on the appearance of a son, and it is the only religion that suits me and that should be suitable to all suppositories. A doctrine founded on the incomprehensibility of God accounts, far better and far more than any other, for life, for the world, for time, and for suffering. Everything that occurs is the whim of a shouting father. My father didn't go easy. You ran back to your room and you popped your thumb in your mouth as you sobbed on your bed.

"When I was little, like every little girl, I had dolls. I had a favorite doll, with a rag body, rag arms, and rag legs. She was called Agustina. It's the name I had given her. Her head, her belly, her hands, and her feet were made of hard porcelain. I had called her Agustina because the most beautiful woman I knew bore this ridiculous name. She was my mother's little sister; her older sister was called Monica. She would say, laughing, that it was a holy story; that Saint Augustine's mother and her son's name had finally come to terms, like Saint Ambrose and lust, for instance. This joke made her laugh a great deal.

"My nurse had led me to believe that dolls had a soul, that they could fall sick and could die if you just forgot to feed them one day. Every night I woke up in tears, terrified at the thought that I had neglected to give Agustina some bread or a piece of fruit.

"I loved her. The only thing that shocked me about my doll was the way she had of not resisting me. Agustina's head was never straight. Her legs wouldn't hold her up. You always had to lean her against a pillow; and, always, she collapsed. I swore to myself that I wouldn't be like her. She undoubtedly submitted to caresses and to the strangest positions of the body far better than other dolls, but she just held herself too badly. I could pinch her without her yelling: it only caused a slight crease in the pink satin. My mother was already no longer alive when I was at the age when I played with her. I loved the gentleness of Saint Monica reweaving her maternal ties to Saint Augustine, but I would have wished to be a less enraptured and stronger woman than the mother of the Father of the Church."

CHAPTER XI

"I now reach a moment in my life that is distressing to me and that is sordid. I could leave it aside, since it concerns only me and has only to do with the disgust it plunges me into. No one knew anything about it, I believe, other than two people who had every reason not to talk and would have ruined themselves immediately if they had. As for me, I am going to confess it because I have often nourished the desire to since I lived it; there is an allure of uneasiness surrounding the months I spent with Didac that makes me think of the border of light that glazes God's face with a golden film as he is dying on the cross. It is the same with other parts of ourselves, sometimes, when we unclothe them. At least those parts we don't share with the other sex and that make for our unfortunate and terrible destiny. The stiff cocks of men become then—a meter away from the burning fire that authorizes us to shed our clothes—like the heads of church saints surrounded by the nimbus that Rome bestows.

"At the Liceo the house lights were down. We could hear Monteverdi being sung and all the passions of the human soul were there, imploring. I had strong hold of Didac's hand. We were ready to snap from tension. We did not look at each other. We were of course alone in the box, but the boxes at the Liceo jut out far enough to be exposed to everyone's view.

"When we had reached the aria—in Westrup's version—in which the very skinny soprano playing Nero convinces Seneca to die, I pressed my thigh against Didac's. I released his hand and gently placed my hand on his sex. He hastily closed his legs. I waited for him to grow stiff and for his member to quiver. I put my mouth next to his ear and said to him: " 'I can feel your desire swelling and I want to tell you that it is communicating its impatience to me.'

"I lifted my ass and, pretending to maintain a seated position, felt his sex leap under my fingers. Then I released his penis and took hold of his hand again. I nudged the chair aside. I placed his hand under my ass. He did not shy away. I let go of it and let him continue.

"Lucan and Nero were rejoicing over Seneca's suicide. They were laughing in tempo: 'Ha! Ha!' In every creature there lingers a continuation of the abyss God drew it from. This continuation exerts itself, whatever the light cast upon it, whatever the splendor surrounding it, whatever the song that charms it, whatever the happiness it is drawn to, or flees, as is more often the case. Saint Augustine asserts that before the first sin an imperfection was already carrying us away. The sin once there, it incessantly hurls us ever farther into the fear that anticipated it. That's my life.

"Finally I felt his hand creep under my dress. It rummaged in my underpants; it strove to break through the silk. Finally, because I was very wet, the fabric gave. I felt his forefinger moisten itself at my lips and then slide toward the hole, penetrate it, and bury itself all the way in, in a sudden thrust. I nearly fell, for I had not thought my friend would proceed with so much vigor.

"Together, each with a hand clenched on the velvet railing, we watched the young mezzo playing Octavia move toward the edge of the stage. She began to sing the Farewell to Rome aria.

" 'Excuse me,' I suddenly whispered in his ear. 'I can't hold it back.'

"And the water splashed to the floor between my shoes."

CHAPTER XII

"We reproduced a similar scene, or very nearly similar, in a church during Domingo's wedding; not far from my house in Vallvidrera at the little museum, in the Verdaguer room; at the governor's, during a reception, in the library; in the train from Barcelona to Port-Bou, Paseo de la Aduana; in the prison, finally, during a visit of the premises organized by Guerra.

"When I noticed that as I was coming Didac also was emitting and soaking his pants, I forbade him to, because it detracted from my pleasure. I intended for the time being that he think only of me and that it not be of profit to him. He consented, on condition that I set at seven rather than nine the number of pleasures he would have to wait. I accepted. I remember that the second time I came, in the church of Nuestra Señora de Belen, as I was adjusting my clothing after the effusion, my silk panties had been so torn that they fell to the flagstones. Didac picked them up and put them in his jacket pocket. We congratulated the new-lyweds. We left.

"We were looking for the car. I asked him kindly to return my underpants to me. Didac pretended not to understand what I meant. I slapped him. He pulled them from his pocket and handed them to me. I threw the panties in the gutter.

"The day we went to the prison, when we had come out from the Montjuich citadel, I refused to let him drive me home. I was shocked and furious at the large stain on his fly. I came back down alone. Two gypsies, sitting on a pile of stones, whistled at me. I immediately veered toward them. Their laughter ceased at once. I caught sight of a caravan and knocked on its door. No one was there. I went up to the boys without a word, simply holding out my open palm to indicate that I wished to have someone tell my fortune. One of the two boys, with very curly hair and a turned-up nose, rose to his feet. When he re-turned, he invited me to follow him. A woman of around forty, with a beautiful, weary face, sitting on a chair, shuffled her cards and spread them out on her apron, which was stretched across her thighs.

" 'Do you want health?'

"I shook my head no.

" 'Glory?'

"I shook my head no.

" 'Children?'

"I shook my head no.

" 'A long life?'

"I shook my head no.

" 'Love?'

"I shook my head no.

" 'Do you want peace?'

"I shook my head no.

" 'Do you want to know the future?'

"I shook my head no.

" 'Do you want your business to be a success?'

"I shook my head no.

" 'Do you want Paradise?'

"I shook my head no: I told her I wanted to know what it was I was living.

"She fell silent. She looked at me for a moment before turning over a few cards. She said that she saw nothing. That there had once been a grenade. That there would be a toad. But no man figured in my life."

CHAPTER XIII

"We do not know who prepares the effect in its most distant cause. We know our weakness at the time we are suffering, but the suffering remedies it not at all. We know we are going astray when we go astray, but this knowledge doesn't show us the path. Even now, I cannot gather these memories together calmly. I am overdoing it. My tone is too sharp, as if the confession could be made easier by a heightened vehemence. To tell the truth, at that time my emotion was less clear, my hope less defined, my body more blurred to my own gaze, and the remarks I addressed to Didac alike intrepid and timid, without his perceiving it. I remember that he blushed when I spoke, or that he would bring his fingers to his brows as if they were itching."

Then, out of the blue, Elena Berrocal burst into tears. It was so unexpected that I rose to my feet. I took her

43

in my arms. It was only in fragments, between hiccoughs and sobs, that I heard the end of what she wanted to tell me. This narrative, juxtaposed with the memory of what Didac Cabanillas had once told me, seemed clearly tendentious to me. It revolted me a little.

Elena had buried her forehead in the hollow of my shoulder. I could feel her hair on my cheek. I could feel her lips and breath on my neck.

The day of reckoning—the day when Elena Berrocal had to give herself to Didac Cabanillas—finally arrived. They went by car to Elena Berrocal's villa in Vallvidrera.

She entered the room and drew the great velvet draperies. She turned the wick of the oil lamp all the way down. They did not speak to each other. They undressed. She buried herself under the sheets. He was slower to take his clothes off; his shoes were laced; his bare feet left a damp mark on the wooden floor; his stiff member was in the way and got caught in his underwear. He made vain efforts to conceal it with his hand as he joined her under the sheet. After he had embraced her, after he had caressed her, he placed himself between her legs, but his sex had gone limp. He caressed her shoulders and breasts again. He remained for a moment with his face buried in her hair. When she put her hands on his back, he freed himself, knelt by her belly and tried to bring his lips to

44

her fleece. She pushed him away, taking him by the neck and bringing his head back to her breasts. After a long moment during which she caressed his back, she stopped and said, "When I was not disposed to, you wanted to. When I want to, you don't show much eagerness."

"You humiliate me," he said very softly, and turned on his side.

Elena got up and began to dress. She said to him as she was pulling on her stockings, "It's you who humiliate me."

He too got up, and they returned to Barcelona.

CHAPTER XIV

They were having dinner in a restaurant, sitting face to face.

"We are going to leave each other," he said to her.

He suddenly saw that she was shaking in every limb. She tossed back her great mass of black hair, looked him straight in the eye, then turned her face in the direction of her plate.

"I love you," Elena whispered to him.

He brought his hand forward on the tablecloth, took her wrist. Her skin was clammy. He said to her gently,   "But you have no desire for me!"

She didn't answer immediately. Her breasts were rising rapidly. She was staring at him with a look of rapture that made him uneasy.

"What do you know about it?" she said.

"Very simply, you have never put your hand on my

naked sex. Nor has your gaze gone to it. Nor has your mouth approached it."

Elena Berrocal snatched her wrist from Didac's grasp. Her face puckered for an instant, the way little girls' faces do when their parents scold them.

"Stop!" she said.

She refused to say anything else and, for the rest of the dinner, would not suffer him to speak.

CHAPTER XV

Elena Berrocal confided to me that Didac Cabanillas's insistence, his need to pour out into language, into the light, into the air, every thought and every reproach that entered his mind—together with his entreaties, his ultimatums, his blackmails—all of it exasperated her. Just as she was exasperated by the pleasure he took, on Sundays, in carving little modern-style bowls. His perpetual protests made her indignant. When he said: "The thought of you is with me hour by hour. I spend my days waiting for you. I spend my nights. . ." she would answer: "Little does it matter what you think about me when you are elsewhere. Your nights, little do they matter." She couldn't stand having him beg, after he had wounded her. She would have prefered him to decide to go back to sleep at Via Layetana rather than whimper about his nights during which he had so much desire for her because she wasn't there. He continually reminded her of the way their love had started and judged that what she had demanded of him had been more perverse than pure. All the fault, and even his own deficiency, were ascribable to her. Even for the anguish he felt, he called her to account. Her way of life seemed to Didac Cabanillas to be against nature, her conduct very little feminine, her designs unpredictable, her refusal of marriage fearful, her rejection of procreation abnormal, her need to break rules laughable, and her taste for independence tyrannical.

"My life is simple and obscure," she would answer him. "I saw you. You seemed alive. I wanted happiness. I try all the time to be sincere with the impulse that governs me."

But she could not stand his putting her in the position of having to justify herself. One day, as he was bringing his hands to her face and lips, because he liked to trace their contours with his finger, just as he liked to nibble at their substance, and because everything was limited to that, she said to him, "You are the one who was right: there is nothing to be gained from our ever seeing each other again."

She confided to me that she was looking at his hands as she said goodbye. "I was observing," she said to me, "those quarrelsome hands that didn't know how to treat me, that body I loved, those very round dark bags under his green eyes, those soft fingers that no longer even wanted to penetrate deep

49

inside me, and I was driving them away even as I longed for them so much. I loathe squabbling and scolding, and to be shouted at for what I am. I could hear that muted voice and that vocabulary—by turns old-fashioned, complicated, charming, deft, unjust— that touched me so much, and I was saying goodbye to them. Men didn't understand anything."

I caressed her hair. She withdrew her head and, moving away from me, looked at me. She was shivering a little. I gave her my handkerchief just as she began to cry again.

CHAPTER XVI

After she had dried her eyes, she drew completely away from me and sat in the black armchair with the straw seat. She fluffed her hair with both hands. I myself returned to my place on the warm hearth-stone. I shifted an andiron. I took the poker and maneuvered one of the two logs on top of the other. I toyed about with the embers and the flames.

She resumed.

"At that time, my aunt wasn't well. She lived here. This house is hers. That hearth you are sitting on is hers, it is her wood that is burning and you are poking at. It comes from a long and magnificent stretch along the Guadalquivir and is partly got out by water. Those woods, those fields, that shore also belonged to her.

"Much as I loathe the summer, I was amply rewarded for having remained in Barcelona with

Didac Cabanillas, before I broke with him that night I just told you about, by the happiness my constant presence brought to my aunt, who was soon to die.

"She knew everything about me; she had once seen me so madly in love with a man as to reach the point of deciding to kill myself when he left. She had climbed up on a stool. She had removed from her niece's neck—I was sixteen years old at the time—the slipknot tied in a curtain cord. She's the one who took me to see a doctor. She had spoken in vain—without telling me and without breathing a word of it to my father—to that friend of my father who had seduced me and opened my body, only to desert me finally for another woman—far less young, far less eruptive, far less awkward no doubt, far less sensitive certainly. Moreover, I always held it against her: she had no business taking such a step.

"I would join her here at the end of the afternoon. I showed you her room earlier. It's my room. The shutters were closed, but she never let anyone release the loops and drop the curtains. She wanted to hear the sounds coming from the Calle Conde de Asalto. I would sit near her in a straight-backed Voltaire chair and take her hands. I sometimes stayed to dine at her side, with her. She ate dinner as of old, very early, at eight. One day, wearily dropping her spoon onto her plate, she said to me: 'My child, I suddenly have a regret as I'm clearing out. I would have liked to have had children of yours on my knees and to have heard them trotting around me . . .'

"I must have interrupted her, shaking my head and letting out a groan, for she said, " 'Let me speak, my furious one. You cannot understand me. You want to possess everything; you light in your night the fuses of bombs; you immerse everything you experience in a muteness that probably seems virile to you. . .'

" 'Who are you describing? Are you talking about Gaspar Guerra?'

" 'Let me say what I want to, my child,' she said, taking my hand. 'I don't have that much breath. I can already feel a sort of emptiness creeping through my whole being. I can feel my brain vaster and less focussed. I can feel—I could almost say I recognize it—the distant sweetness of death coming over me. I have the impression of already being far away. Listen to me seriously and without yelling: I want you both to live here. . .'

"I was unable to repress a sob. I had not told her that I had broken with Didac Cabanillas; I had feared it would make her unhappy. She let her head fall back onto the pillow. She lowered her eyelids. Her hand was very light in my hand.

" 'I want. . . But where are you, Lela?'

"I was by her side, crying. I squeezed the fingers of her hand to let her know I was there. She raised her eyelids to glance at me, and recognized me.

" 'I never had any children, my child. I loved a

man who was full of vigor, but he didn't give me any little girls and boys. He did not wish to, and I, like a fool, loved him. I respected his will. I didn't have any children, he loved me; this man loved me very strongly. . .'

"She fell silent. My aunt had never spoken to me of this love. I asked her very quietly, " 'Aunt, what do we mean when we say that men love?'

"She closed her eyes. We were whispering.

" 'The sweetest thing there is, my child, and also the most painful.'

" 'I have only known the pain of it.'

" 'One only knows the pain of it. The joy is simply the normal functioning of the body; it is hardly to be felt, like a thing that comes when it is due. And, as it is a functioning, it is a mindless thing. And, as it is a functioning, it leaves no trace of itself behind and can never be known. Forget him!' she finally said to me. 'It's such a long time now that I have been telling you to forget!'

"Then, I was fifteen and a half. He was an engineer who was about to turn forty, trained at Cuevas de Vera, and who ran a dynamite factory. He had very long and very beautiful hands. It was perhaps also the idea of dynamite that had gone to my head. It is perhaps difficult for me to distinguish love from explosions, from lightning, from the nitroglycerin that lurks inside dynamite, from unreasoning terror, from volcanoes and sudden night."

CHAPTER XVII

"My aunt was stout and yet she moved like a wraith: her fat feet, which I have always seen enveloped in beige cotton stockings, barely skimmed the ground. The fat fingers of her hands reached nimbly for a glass, the switch of an electric lamp; they brushed my hand gently and knew how to soothe me.

"She had long ceased to return her friends' visits. She no longer did much other than read and die. She sometimes listened to music on the hand-cranked victrola she had in her room, but more often, when she had to get up to relieve or wash herself, she would make her way to the living room, puffing, and would sit for ten minutes at her harmonium. I introduced her to Webern—whose scores Didac Cabanillas had hastened to give me after he had introduced me to him and seen my enthusiasm—and Webern, played by me on the harmonium, made her scream and even shriek with laughter. I laughed too, so hard that I had to stop playing. It was our last good laugh together, but a truly good laugh—boisterous, interminable, hurting the chest and belly, ending in tears—a truly crazy laugh during which my aunt even peed a little, to the point where we had to change the lined yellow flannel dressing gown she had put on.

"She always wore thick beige cotton stockings that wrinkled at the knees. She had lost a lot of hair. She dyed what was left with juice of cashews that brought out even more the shiny surface of her scalp. She encouraged me to have fun, to eat, to enjoy, to live so long as the body could keep up. She found me beautiful."

CHAPTER XVIII

"Curiously, my memory wouldn't let the image of Didac's body fade away. This man, inexplicably, pursued me in the form of sadness. I had been told that he was wandering about Barcelona, alone and haggard, and I blamed myself for it. Juan, Laura, Thommaso, Jordi had seen him at Guerra's: nothing could be more poignant, Juan said, than the face of a man who is suffering and who is containing what he is feeling; of a man who is obsessively striving to distract you from the impression he is making. Juan expounded the following idea to me, according to which the sight of a man repressing a sob distressed him more than the face of a woman holding back her tears, because the sight of a man weeping is more repellent; because it awakens more fear that a graver breakdown may be threatening; because it provokes anger or exasperation in the face of so much weakness. I retorted that a woman in tears exasperated me in the same way. Juan found Didac better looking for having lost weight. I retorted that I didn't particularly favor men being skinny, like underdeveloped children further starved by their adolescence. Juan replied that, in any case, a man is less apt at managing his tears' behavior than a woman has learned to be. I gave a contemptuous shrug. Thus—he continued—when he had seen his lips tremble, when he had seen his chin involuntarily tremble, he had felt heartbroken.

"I was heartbroken. I told him he was spouting tripe and threw him out. I remember that I immediately turned to the mirror that was set in the portmanteau standing in the vestibule of the Via Layetana apartment. I tried my skill at making my chin tremble. But my tears got there first. I looked at those grey drops, that long face, that stubborn brow, those thick and cracked lips, those great dark eyes, that overly grave expression, and that long neck. I thought to myself that I had never understood anything at all about my face. I had no idea what it said, but in any case I had never been what it said. It was an incomprehensible sign in my life. I found and I still find that my breasts are too big, my hips too broad. There was then something about my body that filled me with wrath, and also with a feeling of injustice. Without having grown used to it, I have resigned myself to its strength, but it has also become more useless. I have never completely understood how men could have wanted to possess me. Had I been a man, I wouldn't have been taken with myself.

"Spite adjoins hatred. Sensuous, aroused to the point of madness by the attraction of anything forbidden to me, never, in the arms of any man, have I been fulfilled. And my cunt, under the effect of their hands or the thrusts of their sex, remains as dry as the desert.

"I remembered Didac Cabanillas holding his drawers in his hand before placing them on a chair, vainly seeking to hide his straining penis. I pointed out to him, " 'How damp your feet are from having been squeezed inside your shoes! And how frail they are on the floor.'

"The sight of those dark prints on the wood fetched up more joy within me than his hands on my skin.

"I left the mirror. I felt that the company of Juan, whom I was seeing again, was something I couldn't stand, that a knot is retied in the same way and with the same strength, that the pain with which I thought back on Didac's hesitant body was still just as acute, that I wanted no further dealings with men. . ."

Elena Berrocal turned toward me, her gaze questioning, but I said nothing. Still gazing at me, she confessed that she had hardly touched a man since that day. Over against them she had set God, the Christians' god, that is to say a violent, lean son, full of anguish, inconsolable. A son of God whom the idea of dying terrified. A son who paled at the sight of the least nail. A son racked by insomnia. A god whose mouth was full of vinegar. She no longer desired human men because she detested the pettiness and frequency of their desires compared to the intransigence and the absolute character of what she coveted. Men were assiduous. Assiduity was unbearable. She detested the quest for success or glory; she hated the attraction of money; she had contempt for the diversion of art, the foolishness of colors, the doltishness of sounds, the dupery of words; contempt for the competition of envy, for fratricidal exaltation; for the games of death, of authority, of vanity, of war. For all that, she did not want a father, or a society of fathers, nor did she accept a church, nor did she tolerate submission to a nation. She had finally decided that she was not a woman to give herself to any cause whatsoever. Not even to a man. Not even to his memory.

She had fallen silent. She had looked at the hearth, where the edges of two black logs were being consumed. She exclaimed: "I now feel the regret that gripped my aunt on the eve of her death! The children of men are magnificent. They are more alive than their fathers are. And if I have ceased to grant myself whatever joy I please, it's also because I was repelled by having to be a slave to it."

She placed a foot on the andiron I had moved and pushed it farther back into the fireplace. Upon doing that she said:

"One would probably not be so opposed to what ordinarily gives pleasure if it weren't for children. You cannot understand. You are not a woman. Children take fifteen to twenty years to grow up and they devour our days. They are a joy whose consequence is too long and throws us into old age without our having had any respite.

"Nonetheless, I wish I'd had six children."

CHAPTER XIX

"Have you ever thought of what was happening to Didac in the meantime?" I suddenly asked her.

This question had been torturing me for three years. I had no idea whether she even knew he was dead. I hesitated to tell her without knowing more.

"Oh yes," Elena Berrocal retorted, "I often think of Didac. I often have a thought for the man who most shared in my life—but through the mind—and who probably didn't realize it. Yes, I have thought about what would have tormented him. About this strange challenge that had led me to love him, and which perhaps turned him away from me. Better than most I know how difficult it is always to hold back your cry and to reach your climax silently.

"That challenge, which had brought us closer together than tenderness would have done, left me alone.

"In order to calm, to divide, to temper, to damp the sensuality I am made of, just as the sisters ordered me to do when I was a child, I have fasted at night. Before going to bed, I have steeped my soul in music on my aunt's harmonium, above all in knowledge, at least in studious reading. I have prayed. I have done humble tasks. For instance, I washed the fish basin in the patio after emptying it and transporting the slimy and leaping creatures in great clay pots full of fresh water. I still do a great deal of cleaning. What I mostly call 'praying' is contemplating, drinking a cup of coffee, getting down on my knees, daydreaming without doing anything, reading. Dreaming is perhaps even more praying than praying—at least when you don't hate your dreams or don't expel them from the homeland of your desires by holding them to be nightmares. Time doesn't exist much.

"In a few days I was back at the age when men, like food, fill girls with a terrible disgust. A long time ago, this terrible disgust vanished as if by magic under a carriage gateway when my drawing teacher, an old voyeur, with an apology, abruptly lifted my skirt, drew down my panties, caressed me between the thighs and buttocks one spring day when the sun was warm, contemplated me, was unable to ejaculate, and fled in shame."

CHAPTER XX

"The light was on in the living room. Her head and strands of dyed hair resting on the keys of the open harmonium, my aunt sat on the carpet with the red diamonds. I pulled her dressing gown down over her bent legs and her thick flannel stockings.

"I sat down, beset by queasiness. I fought back a kind of indigestion from the acrid saliva that had filled my mouth, then fought to recover a kind of balance. I stood up again and hastily left that floor of the house. I went to get Domingo and the maid. They came back with me. The three of us tried to straighten her out; the muscles of her knees resisted. Eulalia and I undressed her, washed her, dressed her again. I feel repulsion at undressing and dressing the limbs of the dead.

"I had to go out again to buy a bra suitable for the darkness of the grave, as I couldn't find any in her drawers that would do. Eulalia, suddenly afraid, wouldn't go. God is cruel.

"God is cruel. His image is mute. Nailed hands do not caress."

CHAPTER XXI

Such was the version Elena Berrocal gave me of her affair with Didac Cabanillas. Her confidences did not fit at all with the image I had of her—and that most of her friends, furthermore, had preserved of her. Three years before—one month after Didac's death—we had seen her drop a firecracker into a stove at Moria's to give everyone a scare, to laugh too, and with the purpose of breaking the understanding that had just been reached. She had lost weight. Her face was nigh to ravaged—if one could have eluded the violence of her eyes: they were darker and more intense than ever. She was methodically, unsmilingly, using a lace handkerchief to clean from around her fingernails, from the back of her fingers the soot left there by the stove lid she had lifted up. I was careful not to go near her. In our eyes, Elena Berrocal had always spent her time weaving inextricable intrigues,

66

had always excelled at embarrassing the powers-that-be. But I was not the only one who envied her for having remained faithful to the times when we set bombs. I immediately left Moria's house. I was thinking that a man could die because the woman he loved would not caress him.

We also admired her for the way she dressed. She wore every possible outfit in the most natural way and with an almost imperious manner. She could put on grass-soled espadrilles and cover her head with a linsey-woolsey cap as Saint John of the Cross used to do. We would laugh.

When we had known her, she had a passion for films. Accompanied by her aunt, she had gone to see everything between 1912 and 1914. She already liked to whirl and leap on the dance floors of the Calle del Cid. She claimed that she inherited this violence from her father's grandfather, who had commanded a resistance group during the French occupation. He had been shot by the French in 1809.

Politically, though she was Guerra's mistress, I don't think she was as Red as she claimed. She was against everything. In fact, on a good many points, her childhood thoughts and what she must have heard said by members of her family had left their mark on her. In her remarks one could make out the antiliberal theses of Mane y Flaquer. She was a secessionist, against the vote, advocated abstention even with regard to Maciá, denounced every form of state. She stayed married for seven months. After having abandoned her husband and still a very young woman, she participated until '23 in the terrorist attacks and helped the strikers financially and personally.

Her maternal grandfather had made his fortune in cast iron. Her father worked for Hispano-Colonial. He had pulled out before the collapse of the Bank of Catalonia. He died during the war, in his bed, his fortune intact. In reality, she was an anarchist. If this word means anything precise, that's what she was. Every God, every government, every general, every father, every priest, every language was her enemy.

She was for the *fueros*, for the *gremios*, against the revolution, against the monarchy. She was for Queen Maria-Christina. She was passionately for every plot, against the absolutists and the royal guard. She was for women's free-masonry, for the Tragala, for the hotheads.

She played tennis at the Turo. Superb and rebellious, alone and unfair, violent and unhappy—this is how we saw her.

She shocked us with the crudeness of her language. The most shocking sexual metaphors abounded on her lips even as she preserved the old patrician manners. She was a patrician. She didn't have a car. She owned a horse. She held herself arrogantly erect on her horse. She would lead her horse to church on Saint Anthony's day, for the priest to bless it.

CHAPTER XXII

Didac unburdened himself to me just before his death. I was already living at the Hotel Falcon. It was the tail end of an evening, at the hotel bar. It was very late. I was very weary. He had told me that he no longer slept. He thought a curse had been put upon him. A loss in the December elections, an impasse in a love affair I knew nothing about as yet, keen suffering due to cysts in his mouth, the banking crisis—all stemmed, as he saw it, from the same plot aimed at annihilating him. This story dates back quite some time and I will reconstruct it as best I can. After his death the sorrow I felt over the loss of this friend was total; it was far more painful than I would have suspected had I been in a position to anticipate the course of events and the tragic suddenness of his end. He was then taking opium, in the form of lozenges, opium to relieve his dental pains; we were drinking alcohol; we had taken off our ties and arranged them artistically on the table, near the glasses. This is roughly what he told me.

"A man let himself go under for an absurdity. A man undid himself by loving a woman who wanted her underpants torn in public because this opened her to desire. What woke excitement in this young woman wasn't what her lover's heart might be feeling, but the sound silk gives out when it tears.

"It can happen that desire abandons you as a result of holding your satisfaction in check. I won't tell you her name. I now understand in a physical way why every love is a story in the past tense. I know now why all men are doomed to bother their friends with the confidential tale of their amorous adventures. You aren't listening to me. You're asleep. You're the only friend I have. Every love is a story in the past tense because it is impossible, in the moment itself, to convey through words the reality of the body under the stress of desire, the reality being wrought within the soul by desire. Because desire is intolerant of postponements. Because desire rushes toward the impatient embrace. And because words immobilize, because language renders things distant, and only exerts its full ascendancy retrospectively, once time has gone by. Love, as soon as it is told, is already no more than a nostalgia, and its name is already ash. Men in love will always be right to prefer silence. To express your love is already to say farewell.

"This woman, now, was frozen. It was more than ash, an icicle of ash. It's the stone in place of a heart that Ganivet speaks of. I don't think she liked Ganivet. I never understood that state of melancholia she would suddenly withdraw into. This coldness has remained within me in the form of pain. I do not believe that it was pure clumsiness on my part. She took pleasure in this withdrawal. I think that she nonetheless suffered cruelly from that solitude. She had extraordinary beauty, dark eyes more intense than anthracite, which shone more than Oriental lacquer, an intelligence so rapid it left you standing still, an intuition that made you blush, tortured lips swollen with sensuality, swollen with pitiless judgments and expressive pouts. I am convinced, even though nothing gave me occasion to think so, that she suffered from this somber independence in which she she had inexplicably committed herself to live.

"The natives of the city of Barcelona have always struck me as equally crazy and inexplicable. The Phœnicians, the Carthaginians, the Romans, the Goths, the Moors, the French, the Austrians, the Spanish have never succeeded in subjugating them after having seized their walls. This city is the rebellious city par excellence. This woman was the rebellious woman par excellence, perhaps.

"She was pure vehemence, pure impulse. You sought to induce her to do this or that, it was enough to turn her definitively against it. She hated everything. She hated communism, nationalism, what she called individualist putrefaction, or again the return to nature, or what she termed bourgeois morbidity. Then, we were both, the two of us, as effervescent as the Weimar Republic about whose freedom we were enthusiastic.

"I met her at a ball. Then I saw her in the dance-halls of the Calle del Cid. You remember how I had enlisted, like a fanatic, in Guerra's team. Guerra lived with her. I was flabbergasted by this woman whom Guerra didn't intimidate. She stood up to him with a force that impressed us all and made her magnificent. I fell madly in love with that great mass of black hair that would fly in anger. At other times, her eyes blazed not with wrath but with a strange terror. She was tall, massive, always stood very straight, as if she were afflicted by a stiff neck that never went away. Her breasts were very pronounced, and she concealed their size beneath a black shawl she constantly drew over them.

"She seemed to have just descended from another world. She seemed only to be tarrying with you during a brief stopover, the time it took to change trains, and would leave you nearly at once. She had a deep voice and great, incongruous laughs that shook her shoulders. It seemed as if she herself did not quite know where she was, or when she was living, or who she was. She gave the impression that the terrestrial world was a small lost suburb, several thousand miles away from the center, where a few bumpkins lazed about, like Cervantes or Heinrich Mann. She wore an old signet ring that was too big for her finger. Aside from constant fright, her face bespoke the distinction, you might have said, of a chevalier out of a novel, just as her lips expressed the avidity of a carnivorous beast, constantly revealing very white, very long teeth when the moment came to incite to riot or to howl with laughter.

"I beg you, I implore you, Blas, pretend you don't know her name. Pretend you haven't guessed it. Her pubis was as black as her eyes. She had ankles I loved, very heavy and white. As soon as she was home, she took off her shoes or pumps. She placed two very solid feet on the floor or on the carpets.

"I recall a photograph she had on the desk in her bedroom and that she refused to put away. It showed her at the start of the Great War, in Constantine, with her mother's sister, who had partly raised her. When she was two years old, her mother had died while giving birth to her brother, Milio, the actor. In the photograph, she must have been fifteen or sixteen. She wore a pleated dress trimmed with lace-work and braid. She stood very stiff, very straight, next to her aunt, who herself was wearing a great tango dress. In the photo the aunt was smiling gently and tenderly holding Elena by the shoulders. Elena Berrocal had in this photo the features of a Medea full of fury. She was thrusting her head forward like a bull about to charge. What seems amazing to me is that she cared to keep in front of her eyes, every day, such an image of herself, with such an ungainly appearance. You would keep running into this brown and cracked photograph on her dressing table, or on her secretary, or on the low table in the living room."

CHAPTER XXIII

"In the vast apartment she lived in, there was hardly any furniture. A big cast-iron looking glass in the vestibule and a chipped table to eat on in the immense living room, hidden behind a screen. The bed with its four black posts in the otherwise empty room was surrounded by long green percale draperies. All this was very dusty and even a little sticky to the touch. I am forgetting the fringes. An enameled chamber pot stood in front of the bed, even though the place had all the amenities. It was Azorín's red umbrella. That was about all.

"At the base of the walls were stacks of books, German for the most part. She hated the French even though she knew the language. This is how we discovered that we had both attended, though we didn't know each other at the time, the worthless lecture André Breton once gave at the Aveneo. Her passion led her to the magazine *391*, to *L'Age d'or*. She would repeat Huidobro's watchword: 'Furnish your living room but never furnish your soul.' But the living room was empty.

"On the contrary, this side of the bathroom there was a boudoir with a secretary, followed by a dressing table, followed by a gray wood washstand, followed by an old portable clavier which, owing to missing parts, was mute. These four pieces of furniture stood in a line along the same blue wall.

"She often fainted. When you were concerned about it, when you pressed her with questions, she would say she had the impression that suddenly her blood, spurting inside her, dizzied her and made her fall.

"She despised Larrea. She despised Ramón Gómez de la Serna. She despised Borges. She only accepted strange and abrupt caresses from me in inappropriate places like the Palau or the prison, the Liceo, or the library, or the church of Nuestra Señora de Belen. The rest of the time, she barely let me touch her. She gladly let me take her hands. But as for her belly and legs, I wasn't allowed to caress them. I hardly dared to glance at them out of the corner of my eye, when she couldn't see me. She would stand at the big modern windows, or else she would sit on the studded green leather bench she'd had fitted under the window, which faced due west, and would twist her hair between her fingers, without saying a word.

"She had a capacity for doing nothing and for standing, magnificent, detached from everything, for hours on end, that astounded me. If you asked her what she was thinking about, she wouldn't answer. I would go busy myself in another room. I fooled the time away gouging out hardwood bowls with a pocket knife. I read.

"Or else she went out without even letting me know. She was the Anti-Artistic Manifesto become woman. She loved the cinema, boxing, tennis, horseback riding, the racetrack, the 'gramophone which is a little machine.' . . .

"She had a delightful head, solid arms, great soft buttocks. She washed her legs in the old-fashioned way. The maid brought a jug of hot water. Seated on a chair, she washed her legs at length, splashing the water on the floor.

"At night, hurrying in, I sometimes glimpsed her kneeling before her bed, her hands clasped on the sheet, her forehead against the sheet. From the abrupt way she rose when she heard me approach, patting her nightgown as if she had nothing particular on her mind, I could only deduce a prayer she didn't dare acknowledge. But I kept silent.

"She also read Saint John of the Cross. I gave her all the books Unamuno had given me. I loved her hair. I loved to roll her hair in my hands. I didn't dare do it often. At night I drew close and tried to sleep with my face buried in that silkiness.

"It often happened, at night, as we both slept curled up, with our bodies nearly fitted together, that I grew excited. My erection would press against the back of her thigh or between her buttocks. She would immediately draw away from me. I would ask her, " 'Why don't you desire me?'

"She would reply, " 'Who knows!'

"This answer threw me into despair, and this despair mingled with the ache that had begun to enter my sexual parts and arouse them. At night, for hours, I repeated to myself, 'Who knows!' and this phrase became the throbbing refrain of my days. It extended to my life. From a refrain, it became my device. Elena, like this phrase, was hostile to all discussion, consigning my sex to the disgust it must doubtless have more or less aroused in her. To tell the truth, the phrase didn't even have the cruelty of implying this disgust; it subordinated all reason to contingency; it removed all necessity from her avoidance of me. It was an inexplicable whim which concerned the most ungovernable part of oneself. Some evenings, just as inexplicably, she would partly give herself, without letting me reach the point of satisfying myself inside her.

" 'These are pleasant sensations,' she would say. 'But I prefer something that gives me a thrill.'

"Then I began to hear behind every word she spoke the specter of 'Who knows!' This specter immediately reawoke in me the desire to question her so as to get a better grasp of what moved her to treat me in a way that seemed so strange to me.

"Once, Elena said to me in a deliberate way: 'I am a little girl who is more affected by the forbidding than by the thing forbidden.'

"This was of no help to me. She gave me all of Benn's writings. They didn't help me either. I never really succeeded in making out the way her character was put together nor through what interpretation some order could be seen in the different faces she presented and the different decisions I saw her take. I am sure that she was guided by a genuine sincerity, but I have searched, I have wandered in an effort to understand it, and I have never so much as glimpsed it. She would suddenly say, in places that weren't private and where she demanded certain caresses of me,

" 'Wiggle your ass a bit, why don't you. Just take your cue from me.'

"She would try to shock me. In movies she asked for violent contrasts. She praised the impetuousness of Buñuel's and Eisenstein's films. Mayakovski had just killed himself. She couldn't abide any of the gods Guerra swore by: Jünger, Spengler, Nietzsche, Hitler, and Hofmannsthal. She detested war songs and Ottwalt's didactic plays, and Brecht's as well. I believe, actually, that I never heard her sing. She could not stand any of the Mann family, or Lukács' shudderings before the montages and the virulence of art.

"She never blushed. Her forever disorderly black hair made me think of a storm that gathers but fails to break. A storm surrounded her long face, which shone like a burst of lightning. She wore dark stockings, made of a tough, rustling material. They outlined and stiffened the contours of her large legs. They shimmered in the dark. She preferred my fingers to me. She preferred places where she ran the risk of being caught."

CHAPTER XXIV

"It is one evening just before Christmas, we are returning from a restaurant, I can see her stop in front of the first steps of the staircase. She takes off her shoes and goes up in her black stockings, on the purple runner, in front of me, quietly. Wherever she was, she would hasten to remove her shoes and took pleasure in walking barefoot.

"That evening, going up the staircase ahead of me, she was holding in her hands a pair of black shoes with narrow heels, high and pointed.

"Once in the apartment, I presented to her the package I had prepared and concealed behind the yellow jug on the washstand. She sat down on the bed, near the green percale drape, tore the expensive paper on her lap. She looked at the little box without smiling. She didn't say anything. She was winding the gold ribbon around her right forefinger without breathing a word. Elena was left-handed.

"She rose, went to wash. I found the ring later, on the wood of the portable clavier near the ebony table where she did her hair and lightly powdered her cheeks. The ruby, set in gold, shone in the shadows, on the red surface of the wood. She never wore it.

"Everyday was a rejection. I never knew what form frustration would take or at what moment my desire, thwarted, would suddenly clench my hands into fists. But I know now how impossible it is to master the suffering that comes from frustration; everything constantly makes it worse; it is nearly impossible to try to stifle it at the moment it reminds you of your abandonment and plunges you back into the distress of a child crying himself hoarse from hunger. I know how illusory it is to try to prevent it from invading your whole day and even the dreams that conclude it, in which desire avenges itself and in which excitation, far from subsiding, amplifies, hardens, freezes.

"Suddenly, Elena would become charm itself, her eyes would fill with a sort of self-induced languor, she would come close to me and bring her forehead near my neck, between my shoulder and my jaw, and press it there. Then she would say, clutching my hand, " 'Oh Didac! I love you, you know. I love you.'

"I would put my arms around her shoulders. I would risk asking her, in a murmur, and laughing, whispering it in her ear, " 'What proof of it do you give me but abandonment and sexual hatred?'

" 'You're unfair! You're the only one who knows how I am able to come!' Elena would say, flaring up at once, wresting herself from my arms and flinging out of the room.

"Then I would retort, in a still lower voice, to myself, that she was also the only one who didn't know how much I loved to come. And, as had become my habit, I would repeat to myself, 'Who knows!'

"I didn't like to beg. There is never anything in one's reproaches that is likely to melt those at whom they're directed. There is never anything in rancor likely to win sympathy.

"One day, resolved to overcome my fear, I took the risk of unleashing her anger and decided to confess what in me was becoming genuine pain. I said to her: 'First, only a persisting desire tells you you love. Lela, listen to me. Don't just shrug your shoulders. It is difficult to convince a man of your love when you reject him. To make a man understand that you love him when you don't want his body, when you've never taken all his clothes off, when you've never desired or kissed the different aspects his desire can take, is a task that, who knows why, seems to me each day more and more hopeless.'

" 'Then you don't know what love is!'

" 'Is it a feeling?'

" 'It just so happens that it is, Señor Cabanillas!'

" 'I would rather have been in your arms.'

"After two seasons of life together I had the unfortunate notion of eluding her kisses myself in order to teach her how a rebuff can irritate, sadden, destroy, and steer every hour and every action in the direction of death.

"To speak with complete frankness, this vengeance was in no way a decision on my part. It was never my wilful intention to use it for that purpose. It was something over which I had no control. She reacted instantaneously. With the disappearance of her bold approaches to me, with my loss of the habit of approaching her, we ceased to touch each other."

CHAPTER XXV

"She claimed to have a fondness for spiders and flies but she wouldn't tolerate their presence in the rooms. Yet she forbade that they be killed. She captured them with a glass she kept her toothbrush in. She would go into her study to get a postcard, or the childhood snapshot that depicted her making a dreadful face beside her maternal aunt, and she slid it under the inverted glass. She carried the bug with both hands to the vestibule or an open window. She released it into the air.

"The bug would return a moment later. I can say now how much I misjudged this woman whom I madly loved, and it makes my nostalgia all the more despairing. In certain respects, she was a child. In her sleep, her left hand tangled in her hair, she would sometimes suck her thumb very noisily.

"She went to Montjuich to have her fortune told

by gypsy women. I remember that she was obsessed because a young gypsy had found a black sun or a dead sun in her cards. I think that she experienced life in the manner of a dethroned king. The sun for her was God. Silence too. And abandonment and fear were mystical children. You could add Heidegger, Schmitt, whatever ones you wanted. She called God 'the half-hour of silence.' One day she explained this phrase to me. All the vanities of this world, all the worlds in the universe, all the fears in the hearts of beasts and men were one and the same turbulence. 'What is God?' asked Saint John. 'It's about a half-hour of silence in the sky.'

"When she was afraid that the conductor might enter and discover her doing what she was asking me to do to her, she was a child in her confusion and haste. In fact, she couldn't have cared less about being seen in this circumstance by a conductor on a train, and I could feel she was entirely caught up in the clatter and roughness of the ride, and in her own breathlessness. And also in her exasperation, each time, at the stiffness of my member rubbing against her thigh.

" 'Excuse me!' she would whisper in my ear. 'I can't hold it back!'

"The water 'landed with a loud splash between her shoes.' She liked to use that expression.

"Meanwhile, she would be staring at the door of the compartment with frightened eyes. She thought she saw the door sliding open. She asked me in terror if we had misplaced our tickets. My sex was voluminous and she drew back her leg.

"The sun was God for her. She stretched out naked by the basin at the Vallvidrera property and completely accepted that I undress and settle down in a lawn chair or on a mat beside her. We would read for hours. These were good hours, or at least pleasant if not happy ones. When it was very hot, we went down into the valley of the park, toward the great ornamental pond with the blue white-trimmed skiff pulled up on its shore. It was only put in the water for the children, her two nieces and their companions or their little girlfriends. She didn't care about the pale skin that most women were eager to have and that was imposed on the two little girls. Parasols and veils seemed contemptible to her. It is true that her skin was naturally very brown and that it drew far more beauty from reddening and glowing than from the milky appearance or the silken-petal look prescribed by fashion.

"When she spoke, raising herself on her elbow and turning her so intense face toward me, it often happened that a lock of hair had stuck to her lips. She would suck it gently. She relentlessly read philosophers that seemed unreadable to me. As for me, I prefered to dream by slipping into the worlds of the novels that she judged condescendingly, but would sometimes leaf through. From time to time, when she thought I couldn't see her, or when an argument she was reading particularly absorbed her, she put her thumb in her mouth.

"I remember that one day when I arrived unexpectedly at Vallvidrera, not finding her by the basin, I had started down the slope alongside the rill. I had seen her from afar, down below, beside the hull of the white-trimmed blue skiff, behind which we would undress because the neighbors could see that part of the garden. She was lying on the large flat stones that slope into the pond and over which the gardener used to drag the skiff to get it out of the water and turn it over. I saw her slip timidly ahead, naked, her legs together, sliding on her buttocks. Then she sat with her behind in the water. I was careful not to make any noise that would signal my presence. I proceeded cautiously upon the stones of the rapids. She was sitting the way children sit, at the edge of the tiny waves. She had opened her legs wide. Just when the advancing ripple came to a halt and vanished, the wavelets touched the hair of her pubis. She let the water come and go over her. She watched while a little piece of loose moss or some fluff from a waterfowl marooned itself upon her belly. She gazed at the hair lifting under the push of the water. She gazed at the bits of straw or a little empty shell that came to nestle there. With her left forefinger, she played at making them come to settle on the exposed lips of the sex I didn't have the right to possess."

CHAPTER XXVI

"One evening, not in Vallvidrera but in Barcelona, before going to have dinner in the little shanties of the fishermen, we had left the boardwalk to sit on the sand of the city beach, and had fallen silent. The sun had gone down. We weren't hungry so we waited. Rays from the vanished sun still lit up the edges of the clouds. A breeze had come from the sea along with the darkness. Elena had opened her eyelids and muttered half to herself that she was no longer all that warm. She was wrapped in a long yellow-silk jacket, her shoes placed beside her. Then she had just fallen fast asleep, her head on my belly, curling up like a child, huddling in the hope of gaining some warmth by diminishing the surface that the volume of her body offered to the wind.

"Night gradually enfolded us.

"I was staring at the edge of the clouds, which were moving and progressively losing the red-gold border

89

outlining them. I could feel her calm and sleeping breath on my sex. All this was so unusual. It swelled up, in spite of my contrary and sincere will that it not do so, and from inside the cloth of my pants it began to throb against her cheek. Elena suddenly raised her face and hair and plunged her great black eyes into mine.

" 'Please!'

"She got to her knees and then rose. She had her furious look again. For the first time, my suffering was more from hatred than love. My jaw-muscles were so tensed that they hurt. I did not want to speak and express my anger too clearly because I was sure to lose her then.

" 'Elena, I'm sorry. Come back and sit down,' I said, clenching my teeth.

"I reached my hand out for her to come and sit back down next to me. She relented.

" 'I'm cold. Let's go soon,' Elena said.

" 'Two minutes!' I said.

"She nodded, ruffling her hair with both hands as she sat down beside me.

"We gazed at the dark, sighing water. I talked to her about the light that had rimmed the clouds as she had dozed and that had then disappeared. I evoked the fact, alone as we were, alone on the whole beach, of our being in the company of forces ever so much greater than ourselves, of the ocean, time, nature, un-human life. . .

"With her foot, she touched the soft sand of the beach.

"I raised my head. I watched those darker masses advance across the black sky. I watched the clouds float in the immensity, in the silence and in the oblivion.

"Anyhow, I said something to her which resembled that. I continued, " 'The sky. . .'

"She turned to me and brought her finger to her lips, saying, " 'Hush.'

"I stopped talking. I cannot deny I was vexed. She took my hand and added, " 'When you speak of the universe, the universe is ashamed of your words.'

"She removed her hand. I wanted to kill her. I nonetheless, as in all things, acknowledged how right she was. I was angry at myself for having spoken so much.

"She had stood up. She wanted to leave. Of course, at that particular moment, she wanted to go have dinner, but in general she always wanted to leave, to move, to refuse her body, to travel. Novels, friends, polite society, dreams, the beach, and the port of Barcelona were enough travel for me. My greatest journey was perhaps to plunge my cheeks, my nose, my lips into the dark and fragrant and supple mass of her hair. I loved to rub my cheeks, nose, lips on her round and heavy breasts. But unceasingly she sought my mouth, moved my sex away from the proximity of her body, and implored:

" 'Do you love me?'

"And, even as she uttered those words, begging, she had nonetheless not ceased to leave me yet again in order to shut herself up within rages and silences that left me with hatred, because I never shared their motives."

CHAPTER XXVII

"I think she suffered from very strong melancholic attacks that her moody and violent reactions tended to screen. She believed in permanent war, total mobilization. As for me, I would recite to myself Jiménez's line:

The trees are not alone, they are with their shadows.

"She was convinced that the human heart is an abyss of baseness and in her view it followed that one had to remain, as she maintained, in the cold and the night of a naked chapel, seated in the most complete silence on a straw chair near a grille, without ever thinking of opening it. God was not a divinity who paired with men. She read whole treatises of disheartened philosophy and obscure theology. She had taken to detesting Klaus Mann because he sided with Benda.

She wasn't always easy to follow. She also had attacks of veritable muteness.

"It was a few days before Easter. Then it was over. The facades of the churches were draped in black. It was very hot. We were sitting cross-legged amid the disorder of the bed. She was smoking cigarette after cigarette. She had been playing solitaire. I was reading. She stretched and said:

" 'That's enough.'

" 'Tired?'

" 'No.'

"She frowned. She had gotten up. She thought a moment. She did her hair, tucked her blouse into the long silk skirt she had spread out upon the bed before reading the cards and said that we wouldn't see each other again. I didn't say anything at first. I closed the novel I had been reading. I picked up the cards scattered across the sheet and put them away. It was four o'clock. She said with a yawn that she wanted to sleep a little. That it would be more appropriate for me to think about gathering my things together than arranging playing cards. That we would dine together that night for the last time, that she was going to give Amalia instructions. What did I want to eat? What kind of wine would I enjoy? That I should think about getting a car to come, to load up everything. That we wouldn't see each other again.

"She dropped her skirt to her feet and went toward the boudoir this side of the bathroom. I got off the bed; I knelt to slip on my shoes and tied the laces. Seized by foolishness, I shouted toward the bathroom how much I loved her, everything I had consented to do for her; I listed all the proofs I had given her of my devotion, all my gifts to her, all her rejections of me. Not once had she been willing to have me come in her mouth. She stood facing me, a washcloth in one hand.

" 'You are making up the bill?' she asked me with contempt.

"She went back toward the bathroom. I called out that everything could be different, in a stammer I described the life we needed to lead. I said that we should move. That we should conclude whatever agreement she wanted. That I would be able to curb my desire. That I promised never again to have any designs. That we could have separate rooms.

"I had rejoined her in the boudoir. I grabbed, on the little gray table, the jug Amalia had filled with warm water. I lifted it, brandished it, threw it to the floor. The jug landed on the black marble with a loud crash, exploding into a thousand pieces of yellow earthenware. There was a great luminous spray. Elena had put her hand over her eyes and was shaking.

"I raised my eyes, looked at her sideways, asked her to forgive me.

"There was a silence. Then she slowly murmured that my outburst was stupidity itself. That if a man and a woman had to live together only to be separated during their sleep, they might as well be separated by space or time or death.

"She fell silent again. She turned her back to me and went into the bathroom. She returned. She was drying her face, rubbing her eyes very hard. Approaching me, in an implacable voice, quietly stressing each syllable, she continued in the same even murmur: " 'You will never be other than you are. I will not be different. I do not like the way I am. You cannot change any more than I can change. You will not become a woman. The sun will not lose its way above us. It will not suddenly be absorbed tomorrow into the sky. The sea will not force its barriers and will not come tomorrow morning to swallow up the Plaza de Catalunya. It will not go and swallow the little tears I see running down your cheeks. Nor the peaks of the Pyrenees. Nor the Liceo. God never shakes off the yoke of the order and beauty of the world.'

" 'However, things like that exist. They are miracles.'

" 'There are no miracles. There is only fate. God is ordinary like night and hunger. Like the movement of the waves. Like your departure!'

"She turned her back to me and I went toward the little table, seized the chair by its dark posts and raised it. I didn't dare break anything else. I no longer had any breath left, nor the slightest strength. I set it down and shoved it back under the table. I went into the second living room to sort my shirts, which were folded in the wardrobe; my eyes were wet. In the second living room, I found I was so weak that I had to sit down.

"After I had picked up the bags in the entrance, recovered in tears my linen and books, stuffed collars and ties and cufflinks into the paper bags I had got in the kitchen from Amalia, I returned to the room. Elena was sleeping. She looked happy and serene. The sheet covered her up to the neck. Her thumb wasn't in her mouth but a fraction of an inch away from it, the damp nail touching the crimson bulge of the lower lip. She was beautiful. Her long hair was tumbled and sleep had deployed it around her head.

"I carefully sat down on the sheet. I had the desire to wake Elena up. I wanted to say to her, 'Listen, listen, Elena.' My fingers were reaching out on their own toward her soft face. I wanted to say to her, 'Wake up, Elena. Listen to what I am about to tell you. Just as everything could have been so different, everything still could be. . .' I bent over her. I brought my lips to her lips. I felt her breath on my lips. I lifted my lips to her eyelids when she moved, when she emitted a great sigh that made me draw back my face. She was pushing the sheet away with both hands. Clearly she was too hot. With her foot she again pushed the sheet down, piling it up at the end of the bed. And then I felt on my arms, on my chest, along my hips, at the tip of my fingers themselves, a quivering that suddenly made me tremble. It was like a ghostly, ice-cold wave that had been hurled at me, that had engulfed me for months and all at once was receding, leaving me alone and cold and soaked forever. I looked at that long, brown, completely naked body, those wide hips, that black sex, those two rising and subsiding breasts in which I wanted to bury my nose and mouth, and for the first time I perceived that they were forbidden to me, that it was indelicate for me to be there seeing them, that I had never known how to appropriate them, that I had never been able truly to give them pleasure or, if not truly, at least a pleasure that came from me. My body was still wrapped in a film of cold; it wasn't really a shiver, and it was no longer really a wave that had receded; I thought of the sloughing of snakes, of a tight and cold sheath of skin detaching itself from me, or rather that I was coming out of without wanting to; not like the sheath of skin that surrounds the sex and that the sex rolls back and towards its base when desire swells it; a sheath comparable to the clothes falling to the feet of someone undressing very quickly before going to sleep, as he is already falling asleep; a sheath similar to the silk skirt Elena had dropped to her feet a half-hour earlier, before going to the bathroom.

"I mused that God was a half-hour of silence in the afternoon.

"Elena slowly raised her right hand.

"For a moment, the fingers remained suspended in

the air, playing with each other as if they had gone stiff during the preceding fragment of sleep; then the right hand sank back down to her face; it found a place for itself under her cheek; then Elena emitted a little sigh of contentment.

"I rose without making any noise. I resolved to leave without further delay. I silently closed the bedroom door. I went into the entrance, picked up the two brown paper bags, which I immediately put back down. I wanted to say farewell to Amalia and give her a thousand-pesetas note, as if I was afraid of leaving a bad memory of me everywhere in this apartment. Amalia was not in the kitchen. In a dish on the table was a salad with nuts and pieces of cheese mixed in. I picked the little pieces of cheese out of the dish and ate them. There was an open bottle of red wine in front of a crystal bottle. I was tempted to drink, then pushed the bottle away.

" 'You don't love me anymore?'

"I didn't turn. Elena stood behind me. She came up to me. She was still naked and poured herself a glass of wine.

" 'You prefer the other?'

"I nodded out of pure indifference. I found this woman magnificent and didn't understand her. I loved her more than I had ever loved her, no matter what I reproached her for, no matter what resentments she had provoked in me. I watched Elena, naked, squeeze a bottle of wine between her thighs, bend, the veins in her forehead showing, and violently pull out the cork. While she was pouring the wine into the glass, at the moment she handed it to me, I had risen, I had lunged. I ran to the entrance, opened the door, pushed my bags out onto the landing, called the elevator, pulled the gate open, and piled them in, tripping. I left."

CHAPTER XXVIII

"I said to myself: 'Strange are the ways of desire in men. It comes at unexpected hours. Whatever the constraints it brings with it, it is sometimes difficult to provide a fitting welcome to the strangest of guests.

" 'Women would give one to believe that we can control this painful cramp, or else that its appearance at the end of the night is just a mechanical event whose importunity we could sometimes spare them.

" 'It is a visitor, just as it is in them, even if its aspect is more visible. We sometimes hope for it for nights on end. We turn on the light, we read, we look at pictures, we pour ourselves something, we drink, we dream, but it does not come. When it does arrive, it demands its place, it strains within nightwear, it presses against the sleeping woman's thigh. If it is not received very promptly, with joy and with warmth, it is vexed and goes away.

" 'It is a joy that must be welcomed at whatever hour it presents itself. It is an orphan screaming and

101

stamping its feet to demand the breast and the warm milk of its mother. It is a prodigal son returning to his father's house. It is a singular parasite of dreams, of the arts, of nights, of wine, of fingers, of lips, of smells, of secretions.

" 'Nowhere is it a paying guest. Nowhere does it take permanent abode. No one commands it. It deserts, no one knows why. It invades, no one knows when. It can appear during mourning itself.

" 'One must accept not understanding it. And profit, no matter what weariness or awkwardness may ensue, from its unexpected arrival, its unpredictable fury. It is the thing, as luminous as it is rare, evoked by the philosopher who ground lenses in The Hague, and whom Elena read when she wasn't buried in Martin Heidegger's essays. It is the opposite of death, host that often corrupts it but to which it never defers.'

"Our foreheads were not yet marked by the signs of grief. We hadn't yet buried Carnestoltes. I said to myself: 'The real is pressing language to the limit. In music too, in books too, desire holds open house. Would women have a banquet of feelings, of death and of reproduction? Whoever doesn't hold the door open upon desire, shutting it following one or two appearances, is shutting the door upon himself and upon death. It doesn't return. Who ignores it, life ignores.'

"This is what I was saying to myself, in a fury, waiting for a taxi in Via Layetana, outside the door of a brand-new building that I would never open again."

CHAPTER XXIX

I have written with the desire to retranscribe, as faithfully as I could, the sensations and reflections of which Didac Cabanillas had spoken to me before his death. I do not claim to have been faithful to the letter in relating what he confided to me. I did not even find within myself the muted sound of his voice, the expressions, the desuetude, the staccato rhythms I loved. As for the sentiments Elena Berrocal was in possession of several years later, as I listened to her speak they presented, to my great surprise, a mystical tinge I found disconcerting. She spoke about some other god. Night had fallen long before. We were in the dining room, and she, Elena Berrocal, was standing in front of the window that gave on the night. She was holding a glass of tawny wine. Here, too, I am reconstructing as well as I can what she confided to me in her effervescence—and some tipsiness, as we had several times helped ourselves to the wine. Her right hand, its nails trimmed short, was resting on the windowpane. Her voice had grown deeper. She had her back to me. She was slowly saying: "God is that which never stops falling. He fell from the sky to the earth. He fell from his mother's uterus to the cold straw in a stable. The skin of his cock fell under the circumcising knife. The carpenter's plane, the donkey on which he rides, the ignominy of the torture, the moaning of thirst, the flesh of the shoulders and the backside torn by the whip, the eyes covered with the phlegm the Jews spat into his face—these too were falls of his. The sadness of the soul, so deep it wants to die, was more infinite and more painful than the cry that fear tore from him. He was placed in the obscurity of the tomb. Finally, he fell to the lowest place, into the sojourn in Hell, during the whole of that long, dark Saturday.

"What is God? That we be born. That we be born from others than ourselves and from an act where we weren't present and where these others were naked. And they were so stripped of everything and so incomplete that they were striving, gesticulating, to be joined, and so pressed by desire, and so clumsy, that they were moaning to succeed. We are the fruit of a jolting between two naked and shameful, brawling pelvises.

"Our tree is a spasm. And the tree is never alone: it is always in the company of its shadow. We still retain something of that lowly origin that surrounds human consciousness with nothingness, that limits its birth in time and restricts its duration. We are never in glory with ourselves. The rebellion that drove the first woman toward the first fruit, in the shade of that first tree, to defy God's interdiction, commands us forever."

CHAPTER XXX

One day after they had left each other, Didac Cabanillas had gone to Vallvidrera. He had wandered around the villa Elena Berrocal owned there. He had walked for hours. He had returned to Barcelona on the Tibidabo funicular.

Towards three o'clock, he had finally made up his mind to enter the park by way of the rill, had sat near the pond, had leaned back against the blue hull of the skiff.

He had walked back up amid the cactuses, had idled about till nightfall. He walked without pleasure. The entire time he wanted to go away, to take leave of himself, to die. He had the impression that for each part of her body, Elena's, a part of his body, Didac's, was weeping. Even for her legs. Even for her teeth. Even for her knees, even for her ankles. He lingered on. He was convinced that at any moment he would see her. He didn't see her.

Strange, this desire that ignored time and space, this recollection of a jug smashed into brightly lit pieces that rearose again and again in his memory as a gesture that might have been crude, or that might have been murderous, and from which he should have refrained.

Didac Cabanillas did not dare to enter Elena Berrocal's house. Yet the shutters and the windows were open. The hedge was taller. The lawn had grown thick. The house was calm and silent. The shadows of the trees spread and little by little climbed the wall of the facade.

He hung about there idly for half a day. "What an attachment!" he kept repeating to himself. He was finding himself chained and felt the desire never to leave, to remain there, in that grass. "It's an invisible rendez-vous," he said to himself. "I am caught in the net of an invisible rendez-vous!" At least those are the words he confided to me.

He wanted to speak out loud, and then to speak very softly, to utter only one and the same sentence: "No, Elena, you are wrong. We love each other. We loved each other. It was without respite, it was constantly an invisible rendez-vous."

Didac admitted to me that he had a nickname for Elena Berrocal deep in his heart: "Face of woe." The last thing he said to me was that she was the one he had been looking for his entire life. And that she hadn't wanted him. That she was the one he had been searching for all the time. And that since she was there, on earth, but didn't desire him, time had become useless.

He returned by the funicular. Two days later, he came to my place and threw himself off the balcony and crashed to the street. He had taken his jacket off as he came in and draped it across the back of the brown armchair in my bedroom.

One day, they had accidentally run into each other in front of Guerra's house. He had rushed toward her in a manner, he told me, that hadn't been very adroit but was irresistible. Elena Berrocal, splendid in a long dress, in a bronze green dress, as blunt as ever, had sent him on his way.

"Adieu, adieu," she had said to him. "It isn't your fault. It wasn't you. It was only the light of my eyes that made your face shine."

CHAPTER XXI

After the evening when Elena Berrocal confessed to me the shameless vagary she had been subject to at the time she loved Didac Cabanillas—a vagary about which I must admit that Didac had hardly been loquacious, or which I had been unable to understand clearly from the little he had told me—I saw her only once again. Still at Calle Conde de Asalto; I never went to Vallvidrera.

When I had left her, she was so distraught that I hadn't had the heart to compare her recollections point by point with what Didac, for his part, had related to me of their love. Nor was I bold enough to ask her what she knew of the circumstances of Didac's death, whether she even knew that he was dead, whether she knew that this death had occurred at my place, or even if he had ever told her about our friendship.

We were on the big Spanish baroque patio. I was

uncomfortably installed on a cold cast-iron garden chair. Elena Berrocal lay stretched out on a chaise longue, covered by a great yellow woollen throw. It was the end of the morning. We had drawn our chairs into the sunlight. She told me that she had been out there from first light, in the silence, in the extreme coolness of the dawning day, or rather in the extreme coolness of the vanishing night. Sometimes she would return to bed after having swallowed eight cups of coffee. Then she sought under the sheets the warmth she had left there. She complained that her body never left any warmth whatsoever behind.

She now lived alone. At night, she said, she was afraid to get in bed; she had the impression that she only had an abstract body left, that she was in the grip of a God who ruled out her ever forming ties with someone. She had the impression that she was the ghost of a child and that she was hungry and that she was going to die. She would pray for a long time before slipping under the sheets. She prayed to the memory of Agustina, with her cotton arms and her porcelain mouth. She said: "Now I have the desire to return to the straw and the manger. I have bought two cats. God can do anything to make us more perfect but he cannot cure us. 'Every virtuous or unworthy act'—our father would say to us in the first days of December, in front of the stucco crèche it was our job to set up on the hearth—'is one of the wisps of straw of the litter on which God will be born in blood.

We must say with David: "Lord, I was before you like an animal." ' We would then sing as we pushed a half-inch forward every night, with our fingers, on the corner of the fireplace, the figures and the kings who—I'm talking about the kings and camels—still had a long way to go. I was seeking then something I didn't know. I am still seeking something that hasn't been revealed to me. Saint John of the Cross says in his Canticle on Night: 'To reach what is unknown, one must first take the path one doesn't know.' This path was a jug of warm water that blew up in my face. Jesus said, 'You will follow a man carrying a jug of water.' I followed a man who threw it to the ground. And, in the same way, this man followed silk underpants that he tore with his forefinger. It isn't in the Gospels, it's in the Bible that God says that sometimes one finds destiny in the lowest and most fortuitous things."

I suddenly asked her if she had known the circumstances of Didac Cabanillas's death. She rose. Her back to me, she said she knew he had killed himself, that was all. I briefly related to her how he had thrown himself off my balcony, as she, crouching, pushed her chaise longue into the shade. She didn't say anything. She stretched out a little farther from me, in the shade of one of the broad stone columns that held up the architrave and the upper cloister of the old mansion. And I, in turn, fell silent. The sun wasn't so strong that it made shelter necessary. I closed my eyes. It gently warmed my skin. I heard her say that between men and women there was no more difference than between mud and mud.

She said then that, in the morning, before the night was quite over, she had to pull on her dressing-gown and wrap herself in the wool of her blankets. Their weight protected her from the cold more than their thickness was capable of warming her. She would put the cup and thermos bottle on the tiled border surrounding the central pool, on which she also put her feet, as I myself had spontaneously set mine. I looked at my shoes then, and at the old moss-covered and nearly gray tiles. She said that she shivered: she shivered without quite being asleep, without quite being awake. She was then like someone absorbed in writing.

She would think about everything and nothing. Sometimes she picked up a book. The air was still so dark that she read with difficulty. She dreamed. She prayed. She maintained that those three verbs didn't mean anything truly precise in the Castilian language, nor anything truly distinct in the universe. It wasn't certain that one could say anything precise at all in the Castilian language. She would gaze, in the fading darkness, at the fat toad that crossed the patio every morning, slowly moving one leg and then the other, always alert, before reaching the ivy and the back lawn. It was like a monk leaving the singing of the matins and returning to his hermitage. It would suddenly stop on the flagstones and remain there, immobile, for a long moment, as if it itself were nothing but a rough stone covered with prickles and brown moss. Then it continued on its way, folding and extending its limbs across the damp and black flagstones. It was on its way to its solitary bed of leaves.

The stars would grow dim. The day, and then the wind, would rise. She could read easily then. She read philosophy books or else Lives of the Fathers. She would unscrew the cap of the thermos and pour herself a new cup of coffee that would immediately be wrapped in steam. At the same time, the clouds were invading the sky. The clouds floated, she said to me, in immensity, and also in silence, and also in oblivion.

I raised my head and pointed out to her that she was uttering a line Didac used to like to quote, he who liked to quote poetry so much. She looked at me.

She leaned towards the rattan table and refilled our coffee cups. She took a lump of sugar. She said that lightning was ever ready to strike, anger ever ablaze, solitude ever certain, fear ever unfathomable.

The design of this book is the work of
Austryn Wainhouse, of Marlboro, Vermont.
It was composed by
American-Stratford Graphic Services, Inc.,
of Brattleboro, Vermont,
and printed by McNaughton & Gunn, Inc.,
of Saline, Michigan.